Welcome to ALADDIN QUIX!

If you are looking for fast, fun-to-read stories with colorful characters, lots of kid-friendly humor, easy-to-follow action, entertaining story lines, and lively illustrations, then **ALADDIN QUIX** is for you!

But wait, there's more!

If you're also looking for stories with tables of contents; word lists; about-the-book questions; 64, 80, or 96 pages; short chapters; short paragraphs; and large fonts, then **ALADDIN QUIX** is *definitely* for you!

ALADDIN QUIX: The next step between ready to reads and longer, more challenging chapter books, for readers five to eight years old.

Read more ALADDIN QUIX books!

A Miss Mallard Mystery
By Robert Quackenbush

A Miss Mallard Mystery

FLAMENCO TO MISCHIEF

ROBERT QUACKENBUSH

ALADDIN QUIX

New York   London   Toronto   Sydney   New Delhi

ALADDIN

An imprint of Simon & Schuster Children's Publishing Division
1230 Avenue of the Americas, New York, New York 10020
First Aladdin paperback edition February 2023
Copyright © 2000 by Robert Quackenbush
Also available in an Aladdin QUIX hardcover edition.
All rights reserved, including the right of reproduction in whole or in part in any form.
ALADDIN and the related marks and colophon are trademarks of
Simon & Schuster, Inc.
For information about special discounts for bulk purchases, please contact Simon &
Schuster Special Sales at 1-866-506-1949 or business@simonandschuster.com.
The Simon & Schuster Speakers Bureau can bring authors to your live event. For more
information or to book an event contact the Simon & Schuster Speakers Bureau at
1-866-248-3049 or visit our website at www.simonspeakers.com.
Designed by Tiara Iandiorio
The text of this book was set in Archer Medium.
Manufactured in the United States of America 1222 OFF
2 4 6 8 10 9 7 5 3 1
Cataloging-in-Publication Data is available from the Library of Congress.
ISBN 978-1-5344-1424-2 (hc)
ISBN 978-1-5344-1423-5 (pbk)
ISBN 978-1-5344-1425-9 (eBook)

For Piet and Margie

and now for Emma and Aidan

Cast of Characters

Miss Mallard: World-famous ducktective

Willard Widgeon: Miss Mallard's nephew and a Swiss police inspector

El Ducko: Famous artist and guardian of ducks in need

Senora Gallina: El Ducko's art agent

Carmen Pato: Senora Gallina's assistant

Manuel Pato: Carmen's father

Lupe Colorado: Manuel Pato's nurse and friend

Scorpions: Notorious robbers

What's in
Miss Mallard's Bag?

Miss Mallard has many detective tools she brings with her on her adventures around the world.

In her knitting bag she usually has:

- Newspaper clippings
- Knitting needles and yarn
- A magnifying glass
- A flashlight
- A mirror
- A travel guide
- Chocolates for her nephew

Contents

1

El Ducko

Miss Mallard, the world-famous ducktective, and **Willard Widgeon,** her nephew, of the Swiss police waited in the lobby of their hotel for their friend **El Ducko** to arrive.

El Ducko is Spain's most famous

artist and guardian of ducks in need. He wears an eye-mask to hide his **identity**. He offered to take Miss Mallard and Willard touring in Seville during their holiday in sunny Spain.

But he was late!

To pass the time, Willard **strummed** on his guitar and Miss Mallard knitted. At last a carriage pulled up to the hotel. El Ducko rushed into the lobby wearing a felt hat with a feather, a long black cape, and his eye-mask.

"El Ducko!" cried Miss Mallard. **"What happened to you!** Your cape is torn and you are covered with dust!"

"As I was stepping into my carriage on my way to see you, a statue fell from the roof of my building," said El Ducko. "I narrowly missed being crushed. I believe it was a **deliberate** act. Yesterday a painting I was planning to sell at public **auction** was stolen. The money from the sale was to be used to build a hospital

for ducklings. **And now this!**"

"Were police ducks called?" asked Willard as he put aside his guitar.

"Yes," said El Ducko. "They are **baffled**. The painting was stolen from a locked room in the gallery of my art dealer, **Senora Gallina**."

"Hmmm," said Miss Mallard. "Take Willard and me there right away to look for clues. I insist."

"Thank you, Margery," said El Ducko. "We'll go to Senora Gallina's gallery at once. It is in her home. Come, my carriage is waiting!"

2

Senora Gallina

When they reached Senora Gallina's, she greeted them at the door. El Ducko explained why they were there.

"I would like to have Miss Mallard investigate the theft," El

Ducko said to the senora. "Nothing escapes her."

Senora Gallina took them to the back of her house and unlocked the door to the gallery. She pointed to an empty frame over the fireplace.

"As you can see," she said, "the painting was stolen out of the frame."

"How do you think it was stolen from a locked room?" asked Miss Mallard.

"Impossible without a key,"

said Senora Gallina. "I keep my house keys with me at all times. **Carmen**, my assistant, whom El Ducko urged me to hire recently, has copies for her own use. What does that tell you?"

"Let me explain, Margery," said El Ducko. "Carmen Pato and her father, **Manuel**, are well known in the world of **flamenco**. We saw them perform at Casa Arturo when we first met in Spain. Remember?"

"Oh, yes," sighed Miss Mallard. "I remember them well."

"Last year," continued El Ducko, "Manuel fell from the stage and injured his back and shoulder and couldn't play his guitar. Carmen refused to dance without him. They were faced with hard times.

"Then," said El Ducko, "when Senora Gallina needed help with the auction, I suggested that she hire Carmen. Carmen is very honest and **trustworthy**. She had nothing to do with the robbery."

"I don't agree!" said Senora Gallina angrily. "She was

in the house alone while I was seeing clients yesterday afternoon."

"What time was that?" asked Miss Mallard.

"Between three and four o'clock," answered Senora Gallina **bitterly**.

"I'll go meet with Carmen," said Miss Mallard, "and see what she has to say."

Miss Mallard, Willard, and El Ducko left Senora Gallina's house and headed down a narrow **cobblestoned** street toward the main street, where their carriage was waiting. They walked next to a high wall with clay pots placed along the top. Willard was behind El Ducko and Miss Mallard, strumming on his guitar.

Suddenly he shouted, **"Look out!"**

He saw clay pots being hurled at them.

Willard swung at the pots with his guitar, and the three of them made it to the carriage without a scratch.

El Ducko asked Willard if his guitar was damaged and if he'd seen who had thrown the pots at them.

"My guitar is banged up a bit," said Willard. "But it still works. And I caught a glimpse of a duck wearing dark glasses and a red **bandanna** on his head."

"This must stop!" said El Ducko.

"My brave nephew!" said Miss Mallard. "Let's move on to Carmen's."

3

At the Patos'

Carmen and Manuel Pato were both at home when Miss Mallard, Willard, and El Ducko arrived. Miss Mallard asked Carmen about the extra set of keys to Senora Gallina's house.

Carmen reached for her purse.

"I have two sets of keys," said Carmen. "One set I keep in my purse. The other set is on the key rack by our front door. The other keys are for all the doors in our apartment."

Miss Mallard **examined** the key rack. She saw that each key was a different color and each peg was the same color as the key. Also, each key had an identity tag attached to it. A green key on a green peg had a tag that

said "Senora Gallina's Gallery."

"What happened the day of the robbery?" asked Miss Mallard.

"It was a **typical** working day," said Carmen. "I was making entries in the account books while Senora Gallina was away visiting clients from three to four o'clock. I was alone except for thirty minutes when I had to run an errand.

"Before I left, all the doors were locked, and they were still locked when I returned. Then Senora Gallina came from her clients,

unlocked the gallery door, and dis-
covered the robbery," she added.

"What was your errand, Carmen?" asked Miss Mallard.

Carmen replied, "Senora Gallina asked me to go to El Ducko's
studio to pick up a sketchbook El
Ducko used for his stolen painting called *The Flamenco Dancers*.
She said she planned to display
the sketches with the painting at
the auction. But when I got to the
studio, El Ducko was gone. I put
a note under his door telling him

what Senora Gallina wanted, and left. The rest you know."

"What did you do after you left El Ducko's studio?" asked Miss Mallard.

"I hurried back, to work on Senora Gallina's accounts," said Carmen.

"Hmmm," said Miss Mallard. "Did you see anything unusual?"

"Now that you mention it," said Carmen, "I do recall seeing a street musician across from the house. I have seen him there before. He

wears dark glasses and a red ban-danna tied tightly on his head."

Willard gasped.

"It's the same duck that tried to attack us!" he said in surprise.

4

Sheet Music

Manuel spoke up and said, "**Lupe** and I saw that same duck on our way to the movies yesterday."

"Who is Lupe?" asked Miss Mallard.

"Lupe Colorado," said Carmen.

"She is a friend. We got to know her when I started to work for Senora Gallina. I met Lupe in the park. She is a retired nurse from Our Duck of Mercy Hospital. She comes to see my father every day while I am at work. She takes him for afternoon tea at a sidewalk café and to a movie afterward. Father enjoys movies."

"When I can stay awake, I do," said Manuel. "I keep falling asleep a lot."

Miss Mallard turned to Carmen.

"Can you tell me more about the street musician?" she asked.

Carmen went to her desk and came back with a sheet of music.

"He was gone when I returned to work, but I found this in the spot where he'd stood," said Carmen.

Miss Mallard examined the sheet of music. On the back, scribbled in pencil, was Senora Gallina's address next to a drawing of a **scorpion**.

Just then the front doorbell rang. Lupe had come to take

Manuel to the movies. Carmen introduced her to everyone. Lupe wore a nurse's cap and thick, heavy glasses. She carried a black leather shoulder bag.

She helped Manuel as he struggled out the front door with his cane. As she did, her bag hit the wall where the key rack was placed. The blow caused the key rack to shiver, and all the keys went scattering to the floor.

"Oh, clumsy me!" said Lupe.

Lupe swept up the keys and put them all back in place on the rack. Then she and Manuel went on their way for afternoon tea and a movie.

When they were gone, Miss Mallard said to Carmen, "The clue you found is a good one. The scorpion on the back of the music points to a **notorious** international gang of crooks called the **Scorpions**. I believe the gang is now in Seville and that they stole El Ducko's painting and that the duck wearing dark glasses and a red bandanna is a member of the gang."

"Zounds!" shouted El Ducko. "That person is in the sketches I did from my balcony of the building across the street! I used the sketches for my stolen painting. They're in the book I keep at my studio. We must go there!"

5

The Sketchbook

Miss Mallard, Willard, and El Ducko rushed to the studio. When they got there, everything was torn **asunder**.

"Done by the dastardly Scorpions looking for something,

no doubt," said El Ducko.

He went to a window and pulled his sketchbook from behind a curtain.

"But they didn't find it!" he said.

Miss Mallard turned the pages of the sketchbook. First she saw sketches of flamenco dancers on the second floor of the building across the street that El Ducko had used as inspiration for his stolen painting *The Flamenco Dancers*.

Then she turned to a new page and gasped. She saw the sketch

of the duck wearing dark glasses and a red bandanna peering from a top-floor window, just as El Ducko had described!

"Good heavens!" she said. "All is clear to me. This drawing shows that you have uncovered the hideout of the Scorpions, which you put into your painting as well. The gang must have read about the painting in the newspapers and stole it to keep their hideout a secret. I must get inside that building to prove my theory."

"We'll help you!" said El Ducko and Willard together.

"But you can't," said Miss Mallard. "The Scorpions have seen you, El Ducko, and know where you live. And, Willard, I need you to stay here. I'll go and pretend to be a student at the flamenco dance school. I'll signal you both from one of the building's upper floors as soon as I suspect trouble. When I do, call the police, Willard. And, El Ducko, do what you can to get me safely out of the building."

6

Down the Ladder

Miss Mallard tore down the stairs
from El Ducko's studio. She raced
across the street, entered the building that El Ducko had painted, and
climbed the stairs to the second
floor.

From the door of the dance school came the loud noises of pounding feet and clicking **castanets**. Then Miss Mallard heard the sound of footsteps coming her way. She ducked into the school.

"Danza!" quacked an instructor at her.

"Oh, but I am not a stu—" Miss Mallard struggled to say.

Before she could finish, a rose was shoved into her beak. There was nothing she could do but join

the others and dance the flamenco.

Miss Mallard danced furiously while keeping her eyes on the door. She saw that no one was passing by the frosted glass, which was a sign that it was safe for her to leave and go out into the hall and continue her investigation.

Once there, she remembered seeing a window at the end of the hall.

She went to the window, opened it, and saw a narrow metal ladder attached to the building. It was a

fire escape ladder that went up to the roof.

It was next to the Scorpions' window!

Miss Mallard climbed the ladder to the Scorpions' window, which was covered with a shade. But the window was open a crack at the bottom, and Miss Mallard could hear the Scorpions making plans to rob a bank.

At once she began waving and hoped El Ducko and Willard would see her warning signal. As

she was waving, she cast a shadow onto the window shade, which was seen by the Scorpions. Suddenly the window shade was raised.

There at the window stood the duck wearing dark glasses and a red bandanna!

Miss Mallard **scampered** down the ladder. Had Willard and El Ducko seen her signals? Had Willard called the police? Above her she saw the gang member coming after her.

Just then El Ducko saw what

was happening. He leaped from his balcony and flew toward Miss Mallard. He reached out a wing for her and flew her back to safety.

Luckily Willard had already called the police a few minutes earlier. At once sirens were heard, and police cars stopped in front of the building where the Scorpions had their hideout.

Policeducks raided the building and arrested the Scorpions, including the duck who'd been chasing Miss Mallard on the ladder.

7

The Solution

Safe at last in El Ducko's studio, Miss Mallard thanked Willard and El Ducko for coming to her rescue and saving Seville from the Scorpions.

"What a relief," said Willard.

Then the three of them went to the street and watched the gang being taken away in police cars. The chief of police thanked them for helping to capture the gang.

"We have everyone except for the leader," he said.

"I think I can help with that, too," said Miss Mallard. "Come with me, and I will line up a list of suspects and reveal the leader to you."

Miss Mallard called Carmen

and asked if she would be home. Carmen said she would be there and so would her father and Lupe. Then Miss Mallard called Senora Gallina to come to the Patos' apartment.

When the suspects were assembled, they were all quacking **impatiently**.

"Quiet, everyone!" said Miss Mallard. "I will explain why you are here. By now you all know about the police raid on the Scorpions and that the leader has escaped. I believe that the leader is one of you."

"How can you say that!" quacked Senora Gallina. "No gang **invaded** my house. One person stole El Ducko's painting. Who did it?"

"Yes, tell us!" said Carmen. "And don't point your wing at me."

Manuel began **trembling** on his cane. Carmen rushed to his side.

"Don't worry, dear," said Manuel. "I am still feeling a little tired. I fell asleep in the movie again."

Carmen turned to Miss Mallard and said, "You see! End this! Think of my poor father's health!"

"I'll be brief," said Miss Mallard. "El Ducko's painting was stolen by the same person who called Carmen to leave Senora Gallina's house. And it was not Senora Gallina."

The suspects were all ears.

"The caller was not working alone," continued Miss Mallard.

"A member of the gang posed as a street musician to check the routine of the house and to be on the lookout during the robbery. He was arrested at the Scorpions' hideout, but he isn't talking. Even so, we don't need him. It is very clear that the caller stole the painting."

"Tell us who called!" demanded Carmen. "I know what I heard, though there was a lot of **static** on the phone."

"Exactly," said Miss Mallard.

"That is the way the caller planned it so you would think it was Senora Gallina calling and asking you to leave the house, so that the robbery could be done."

She turned to Lupe.

"Here is the caller," said Miss Mallard.

Lupe looked shocked.

8

Unmasked

"How dare you!" she said. "I am a respected nurse. I would never do such a thing."

"Nurse?" said Miss Mallard. "You are not listed in any hospital records. Keys are your **expertise**.

I saw how quickly you picked up the keys at the Patos', and I knew you were familiar with them. This was my proof that you committed the robbery with a copy of the gallery key. You took Manuel for tea and a movie, knowing he would sleep during the movie so you could carry out your plan. After stealing El Ducko's painting, you went back to the theater for Manuel, who was still sleeping. He was your cover. **Confess!**"

"Lies! All lies!" quacked Lupe.

"If so," said Miss Mallard, "then let us have a look in your leather bag."

Hearing this, Lupe grabbed her leather bag and ran for the back door.

In a flash, Willard slid his guitar across the room. Lupe tripped on it and fell hard on top of Manuel and the guitar. As she fell, her cap and glasses fell off and her leather bag came open. Out from the bag popped El Ducko's painting rolled up, a box of Sleepy Duck Tea used

to put Manuel to sleep, and a copy of the gallery key.

"I know her!" said the chief of police. "She is Rosa the Horrible. She is wanted for robberies in over seven countries. And now she is captured!"

Quickly the chief of police put handcuffs on Rosa and lifted her off Manuel and Willard's guitar. As soon as he did, to everyone's surprise, Manuel stood up perfectly straight and without the aid of a cane.

"I am cured!" Manuel quacked joyfully. "The blow just now snapped my back and shoulder into place. We can work again, Carmen!"

Everyone was beside themselves with joy, except for Rosa, of course, who was taken to jail.

"Good work, Willard," said Miss Mallard. "But I am very sorry your guitar got smashed."

Manuel reached for one of his guitars and handed it to Willard.

"Have one of mine, Willard,"

said Manuel. "This one is brand new. It is a gift for what you did to save the day."

"How kind of you!" said Willard. "Thank you so much for your gift." He began to play his new guitar.

Swaying to the music, El Ducko walked over to Miss Mallard and said, "May I have this dance?"

"I would be delighted," said Miss Mallard as she clacked her castanets. Together they danced the tango, and they couldn't have been happier.

Word List

asunder (uh•SUN•der): Into parts

auction (AWK•shun): A sale where things are sold to people offering the most money

baffled (BA•fuld): Very confused or puzzled

bandanna (ban•DA•nuh): A large, often colorfully patterned handkerchief

bitterly (BIH•ter•lee): Harshly

castanets (ka•stuh•NETS): A

handheld instrument made of
two small shells

cobblestoned (KAH•bull•stohnd):
Made of naturally rounded
stones

deliberate (dih•LIH•buh•ret):
Done on purpose

examined (ig•ZA•mund):
Looked at closely

expertise (ek•spur•TEES): Great
knowledge or skill

flamenco (fluh•MENG•koh):
A kind of dance that started in
Spain

identity (eye•DEN•tuh•tee): The qualities that make up a person

impatiently (im•PAY•shunt•lee): Not willing or able to wait

invaded (in•VAY•did): To break into without being asked

notorious (noh•TAWR•ee•us): Known for something negative or bad

scampered (SKAM•purd): Ran or hurried away quickly

scorpion (SKORE•pee•uhn): An eight-legged creature related to the spider, with a poisonous stinger at the end of its tail

static (STA•tik): Electrical noise

strummed (STRUMD): Played
an instrument by brushing
fingers across strings

theory (THEER•ee): An idea
why something happens

trembling (TREHM•bling):
Shaking without meaning to

trustworthy (TRUST•wer•thee):
Reliable

typical (TIHP•ih•kull): usual

Questions

1. What does El Ducko wear to hide his identity? Why do you think he hides his identity?
2. Why couldn't Manuel Pato play guitar anymore?
3. What was sketched on the back of the sheet music Carmen found?
4. Where was El Ducko's sketchbook hidden?
5. How was Willard's guitar

smashed? Did he buy a new one?

6. What dance did El Ducko and Miss Mallard do when the case was solved?